TOUR DE YOU

Swirling Circles of Freedom
K.C. WILDER, PH.D.

AuthorHouse™
1663 Liberty Drive
Bloomington, IN 47403
www.authorhouse.com
Phone: 1-800-839-8640

First published by AuthorHouse 11/22/2010

ISBN: 978-1-4520-1099-1 (sc)

Library of Congress Control Number: 2010906397

Certain stock imagery © Thinkstock.

Printed in the United States of America

This book is printed on acid-free paper.

author**HOUSE**®

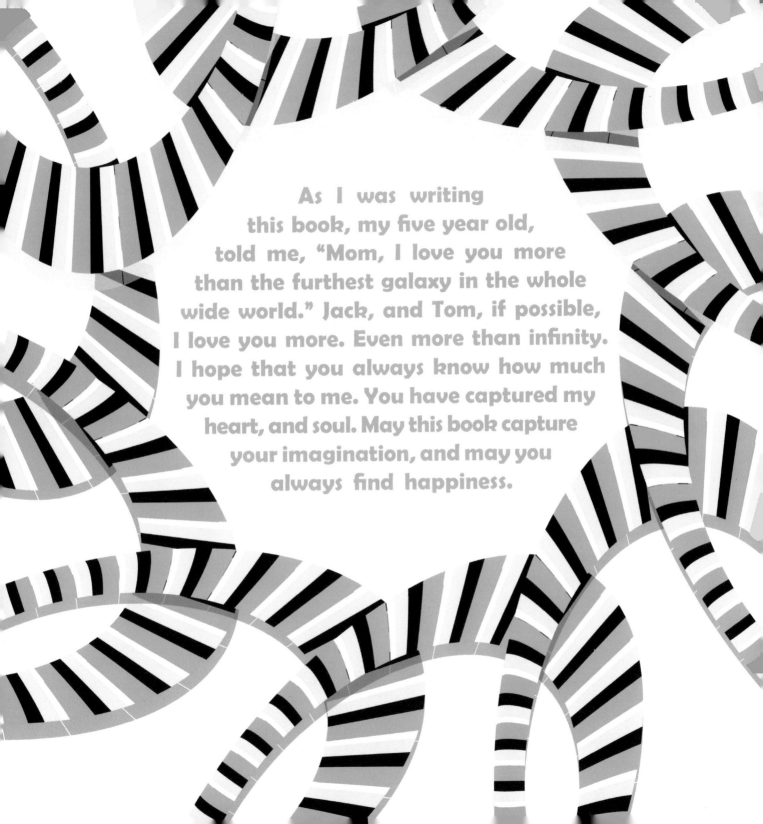

As I was writing
this book, my five year old,
told me, "Mom, I love you more
than the furthest galaxy in the whole
wide world." Jack, and Tom, if possible,
I love you more. Even more than infinity.
I hope that you always know how much
you mean to me. You have captured my
heart, and soul. May this book capture
your imagination, and may you
always find happiness.

Swirl circles of glory,
creating your story.

Set your tempo, and stay at your pace.

You will win your very own race.

Keep turning the sprocket, blast like a rocket.

Keep on your game face,

there is never a perfect race

You may be misled, always use your head.

Be free of fear of success, and never digress.

Your experiences will break you, or give you the freedom to make you.

Keep spinning 'round

swirling circles and free will abound.

Keep on the pressure, dig deeper, stay in the race, and be your own keeper.

You could drop from the from the main group, and crack.
Come unhitched from the peloton, and drop off the back.

**Obstacles will take their toll,
it is best for you to let your tires roll.**

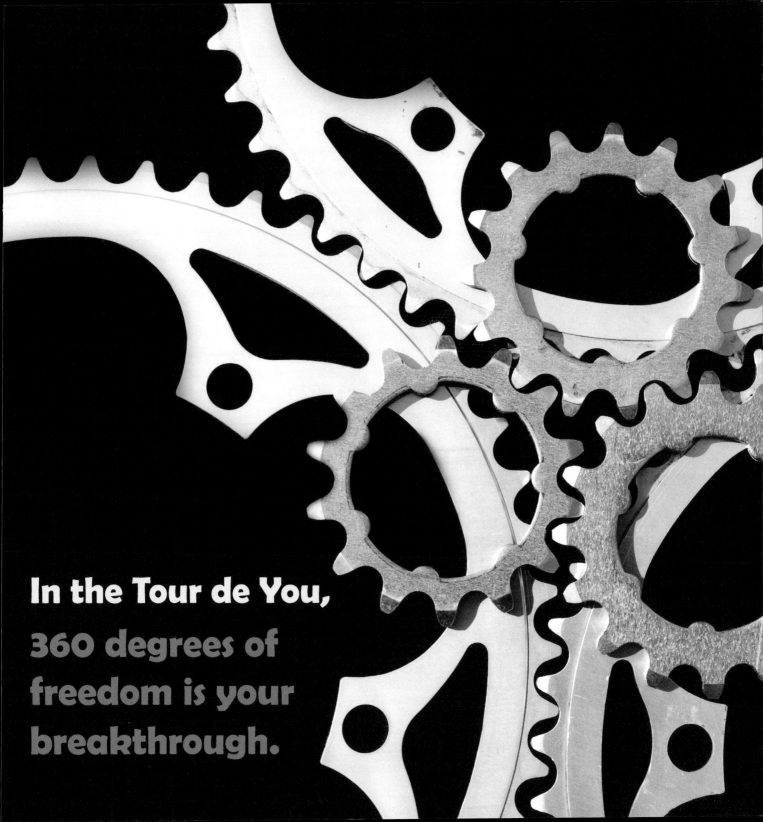

In the Tour de You,
360 degrees of
freedom is your
breakthrough.

Keep up the cadence. Go with the flow,

with this attitude
you will glow.

Reach the summit,

dare not plummet.

Do what you love, and fly free from above.

Strive for the feeling of being on top, and you will never be a flop.

In the end create your own fate, and you will always be great.

LaVergne, TN USA
04 December 2010
207356LV00001B